# The Prince and the Parsnip

Written by Vivian French

Illustrated by Emma Block

**Collins**

Princess Sue wanted to marry
a prince.

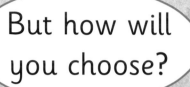

But how will
you choose?

She should choose the most handsome one — like me!

But Sue wanted to find a prince with feelings. She wanted a kind and caring prince.

Sue wrote letters to ten princes.
"Please come and stay in the palace!"

Princess Sue pulled up ten parsnips from the garden.

When the beds were ready, she set a test. She hid a parsnip under each pillow.

Will anyone feel it?

# The ten princes arrived at six o'clock.

At eight o'clock Princess Sue showed the princes to their beds.

Goodnight. Sleep well!

In the morning, Sue asked, "Did you sleep well?" Nine princes said, "Yes."

Prince Tom said, "No. My pillow was lumpy and bumpy. I was awake all night!"

Princess Sue knew that Prince Tom was kind and caring. He'd felt the parsnip under his pillow!

Hooray! I've found my prince with feelings.

She asked Prince Tom, "Will you marry me?" He said, "Yes," and they were married the very next day.

# Finding a prince

# Ideas for reading

Written by Clare Dowdall, PhD
*Lecturer and Primary Literacy Consultant*

**Learning objectives:** use syntax and context when reading for meaning; make predictions showing an understanding of ideas, events and characters; retell stories, ordering events using story language; interpret a text by reading aloud with some variety in pace and emphasis

**Curriculum links:** Citizenship

**High frequency words:** wanted, should, come, eight

**Interest words:** prince, parsnip, marry, feelings, princess, handsome, caring, palace

**Resources:** pens, paper, pencil crayons and pencils, whiteboard

**Word count:** 172

## Getting started

- Explain that today's story will be a different version of a fairy tale, *The Princess and the Pea*. Ask children if they know this story, to create a context for reading.

- Look at the front cover and ask children to read the title. Check that they know what a parsnip is. Turn to the blurb and ask children to read it. Look at the word *feelings*. Discuss strategies for reading longer words, e.g. phonic knowledge, finding familiar chunks within words and checking that it makes sense in its place in the sentence.

- Lead a discussion about what *feelings* are. Create a list of feelings on a whiteboard, e.g. happiness, anger. Ask children to suggest what is meant by the phrase *a prince with feelings*.

## Reading and responding

- Turn to pp2–3. Model reading the text aloud using three distinct voices: those of the narrator, queen and king. Invite children to read these pages aloud, using their voices expressively.

- Ask children to read pp4–5 quietly, then lead a discussion in which children predict how Princess Sue will find a kind and caring prince. Ask children to suggest what sorts of things a kind and caring prince would do, e.g. make Sue breakfast.